SEA
HERO

Steve Barlow
and
Steve Skidmore

First published in Great Britain in 2018
by Caboodle Books Ltd
Copyright © Steve Barlow and Steve Skidmore 2018

A Catalogue record for this book is available
from the British Library.

ISBN 978-0-9954885-9-5

Illustrations by Joseph Witchall
Page Layout by Highlight Type Bureau Ltd
Printed and bound by
CPI Group (UK) Ltd, Croydon, CR0 4YY

The paper and board used in the paperback by
Caboodle Books Ltd are natural recyclable products
made from wood grown in sustainable forests.
The manufacturing processes conform to the environmental
regulations of the country of origin.

Caboodle Books Ltd
Riversdale, 8 Rivock Avenue, Steeton, BD20 6SA
www.authorsabroad.com

BE A HERO!

This book is not like others you may have read. You are the hero of these adventures. It is up to you to make decisions that will affect how the adventures unfold.

Each section of the three books is numbered. At the end of most sections, you will have to make a choice. The choice you make will take you to a different section of the book.

Some of your choices will help you to complete the adventure successfully. But choose carefully, some of your decisions could be fatal!

If you fail, then start the adventure again and learn from your mistake.

If you choose correctly you will succeed in your adventure.

Don't be a zero, be a hero!

SPACE RESCUE

You are the top astronaut at UNSA (United Nations Space Agency). You have flown into space many times. You have also spent several months test-flying new spaceships.

You are the one that UNSA calls if there is an emergency. In the past you've repaired damaged satellites, rescued astronauts from space and even dealt with Alien Life Forms (ALFs).

Early one morning, you are woken by the buzz of your Satvid phone.

"Answer," you say. The video screen flicks on to reveal a worried-looking man.

"We have a Red Alert," he says. "We need you at UNSA HQ immediately. An Agency car is on its way."

"Okay," you reply. "I'll get my things."

You quickly pack your bag and head outside. A sleek, black car is already waiting. You step inside it and the door shuts behind you.

"Good morning. Enjoy the ride," says the car's computer.

As the computer-driven car pulls away, you wonder what danger this new mission will bring.

Now turn to section 1.

1

The car glides to a halt outside UNSA HQ and you head straight to the director's office.

The director of UNSA is waiting for you. "We have a problem," he says.

"And that's why you've called me," you reply. "What is it this time?"

"We have a situation with the UNSA base on the moon," says the director. "Two days ago, we lost all contact with it. We need you to go and investigate. If there is a problem, then you will have to deal with it."

"How will I get there?" you ask.

"You'll fly on your own in the single-seater Dart spaceship," the director says. "It'll be quicker than a shuttle. Speed is important."

You nod. "So I'll be on my own – no back-up crew?"

"That's why we want you for this mission – you're the best. Anyway, it will probably be just routine."

"Or it could be dangerous," you say.

"Will you go?" asks the director.

If you say yes, turn to 46.
If you say no, turn to 8.

2

You hit the fire control switch and the flames die out.

You grip the spaceship's controls tightly and fly through the raging storm. The juddering stops and you realise that you have passed out of the Earth's atmosphere and are in space. You ask the computer to check the instruments.

The computer voice answers. "No major damage."

You make contact with the UNSA mission control. "Everything is okay," you say. "The mission continues…"

Go to 19.

3

You rush into the chamber and hide near the doorway. The alien follows you into the chamber. Before the alien can react, you dash out from your hiding place, and out of the chamber.

The doors shut and you press 'Lock'.

The alien is trapped! It slams against the door, but cannot get out.

You smile.

You will contact UNSA back on Earth and they will be able to send a team to deal with the creature. **Go to 50.**

4

You step into the hangar. Switching on your helmet light, you see a movement next to an oxygen tank.

If you selected the laser blaster at the beginning of the mission, go to 23.

If you chose the ALF detector, go to 48.

5

You tell the professor you have to go, and make your way to the launch site. You head straight to the control room.

The launch controller looks worried. "We have reports of electrical storms heading our way," he tells you. "It could be dangerous to launch. I think we should wait for twenty-four hours until the storms have passed. But it is your decision."

If you wish to go ahead with the mission, go to 41.

If you decide to delay the launch, go to 18.

6

Before you can move, the door opens. You cry out as an alien creature leaps out and grabs hold of you. You feel your mind slipping away as the creature takes over your body. You have been turned into an alien!

You have failed. If you wish to begin your mission again, go to 1.

7

You switch off your oxygen supply and remove your space suit helmet. A big mistake! The atmosphere in the moon base is unstable – you forgot to check!

You are unable to breathe and you drop to the floor, scramble for your helmet and try to turn your oxygen supply back on. It is hopeless. You clutch at your throat as blackness overtakes you.

Your basic error has cost you your life. Go back to 1.

8

The director frowns. "What sort of hero are you?"

"I'm only joking!" you reply. "Of course I'll go."

Go to 46.

9

"What happened?" you ask.

Commander Peters steps forward. "It is all part of an alien invasion plan," she says. "An alien from the Rigus galaxy was sent to take over the moon base. Once it had done this, more aliens would be sent to prepare an attack on Earth."

You look puzzled.

If you wish to ask the commander how she knows this, go to 29.

If you wish to switch on the ALF detector, go to 47.

10

"I'm aborting the mission!" you scream into your radio.

As you press the abort switch, the Dart spaceship takes a direct hit. You wrestle with the controls. It is hopeless. You hear a loud explosion and then nothing...

You have paid the ultimate price. If you wish to begin your mission again, go back to 1.

11

You switch on the communications link. A screen flickers into life and the image of a woman appears.

She begins to speak. "This is Commander Peters, commander of the moon base. We are under attack. An alien life form has been detected. It has been blocking all communications with Earth. It is taking over our —"

The screen goes blank. You realise that this is a critical situation.

If you wish to go to the moon base, go to 43.
If you wish to explore the hangar, go to 4.

12

The meteors keep coming, but you somehow manage to avoid them.

Then as suddenly as it appeared, the meteor storm disappears. You breathe a sigh of relief and report your escape back to mission control.

"Well done," says the director. "Now get some sleep." You turn the spaceship's controls to auto pilot, take a sleeping pill and settle down.

Hours later you wake. The ship is about to enter the moon's orbit. You decide to fly the ship in manually to land as close to the moon base as you can. You have to decide how steep your angle of descent will be.

To land the ship at 45 degrees, go to 25.
To land at 75 degrees, go to 40.

13

Taking your equipment, you make your way to the communications room. You stand outside the door and take a deep breath.

If you selected the laser blaster at the beginning of the mission, go to 45.
If you chose the ALF detector, go to 39.

14

You point at the ALF detector. "I'll take this."

"Good choice," says the professor. "It works by reading the DNA structure of any life form. Now do you want me to go over the Dart spaceship controls?"

"I know all about that spaceship," you reply. "I flew it in all the tests when it was first designed."

The professor shakes his head. "But there have been some changes."

If you want to listen to the professor, go to 37.
If you want to get on with the mission, go to 5.

15

As you make your way across the moon's surface to the base entrance, you see a space shuttle standing outside a hangar. You glimpse a strange figure heading towards it.

If you wish to investigate further and go to the shuttle, go to 33.

If you wish to enter the moon base, go to 45.

16

You pull back on the controls and hit the reverse rocket boosters. But it is too late. Your ship hurtles towards the surface of the moon.

There is a thunderous noise and your ship is ripped apart. You look back helplessly towards the Earth. It is the last sight you see before you plunge into oblivion.

If you wish to begin the adventure again, go back to 1.

17

As you pull the trigger, the alien dodges. The stream of energy from the weapon misses the creature and hits an oxygen tank.

Too late, you realise that you have made a fatal mistake. There is a huge explosion and a deadly fireball engulfs you.

Your lack of thought has cost you your life. If you wish to begin again, go to 1.

18

"It's too dangerous," you say. "We should delay."

The launch controller nods. "I'll tell the director."

Ten minutes later your Satvid phone rings. It is the director. He is furious. "You coward!" he says. "This mission was urgent! I'll get another astronaut to go – one who isn't scared of bad weather. You'll never work for us again. Get off my base!"

Before you can say anything, the director rings off. By not putting the mission ahead of your safety, you have failed. It is the end of your career.

If you want to be a hero, you can start the mission again by going back to 1.

19

Hours pass. Soon, the Earth is far behind and you look out of the window into the blackness of space.

Suddenly an alarm goes off. The computer's loud voice fills the cabin: "WARNING! WARNING! Unidentified objects ahead!"

You look at the computer's radar. There are dozens of white dots on the screen. You are heading straight into a meteor storm! What should you do?

If you want to abort the mission, go to 10.

If you want to switch on the computer's auto flight, go to 44.

If you want to fly the spaceship yourself, go to 49.

20

You stare out of the window. The moon base is about two hundred metres away.

You switch on your com link to Earth. A message appears on the screen:

ALL EARTH–MOON COMMUNICATION SIGNALS BLOCKED.

You wonder what could be causing this and then realise that your emergency communication radio is useless. You are on your own. You are wearing your life support systems and body armour. You pick up the rest of your equipment.

"Open the door," you tell the onboard computer.

The metal doors open and you step onto the surface of the moon.

If you wish to head straight to the moon base entrance, go to 15.

If you wish to look around the outside of the base, go to 28.

21

Using your sat nav device, you carefully make your way along the dark, metal corridors of the moon base.

Minutes pass but there is no sign of life. Eventually you reach the door to the life support systems area. You get ready to enter.

If you selected the laser blaster at the beginning of the mission, go to 45.

If you chose the ALF detector, go to 34.

22

You point at the laser blaster. "I'll take this."

"Good choice," says the professor. "Do you want me to go over the Dart spaceship controls?" he asks.

"I know all about that spaceship," you reply. "I flew it in all the tests when it was first designed." The professor shakes his head. "But there have been some changes."

If you want to listen to the professor, go to 37.

If you want to get on with the mission, go to 5.

23

You prime your weapon and slowly move forward.

Peering into the darkness, you see the outline of a figure. You gasp: it is not human – it is like nothing you have ever seen before.

If you wish to shoot the creature, go to 17.

If you wish to signal it to come towards you, go to 38.

24

You open the door and step inside. The room is full of computer screens, showing the status of the moon base. There are lots of flashing red lights. You realise that you can control all life support systems from here. You sit at the control desk and order the computers to repair and stabilise the atmosphere in the moon base so that you can breathe without your helmet on.

Minutes later, the computers give the all-clear and you take off your helmet. You wonder where the ALF might be and if there are any crew left alive.

If you wish to check the computer for any clues, go to 36.

If you wish to head back into the base straight away and search for the crew, go to 45.

25

Your angle of descent is good.

The spaceship slows down and the surface of the moon gets nearer. You can see the base ahead. You switch on landing controls and fly in. Descent rockets slow the ship down.

You are a great astronaut. The moon dust is hardly disturbed as you make a perfect landing.

Now go to 20.

26

You hurry after the alien, but by the time you reach the hangar doorway, it has disappeared from sight. You decide to head to the moon base.

Go to 43.

27

You pull the trigger. Your aim is true and the figure drops to the floor. You rush forward and cry out in despair. You have shot one of the crew! She must have been hiding.

As you kneel over the dead crew member, you hear a noise behind you. You spin round and scream in terror as an alien creature grabs hold of your head. You feel your mind slipping away as the creature takes over your body.

You have been turned into an alien!

You have failed. If you wish to begin your mission again, go to 1.

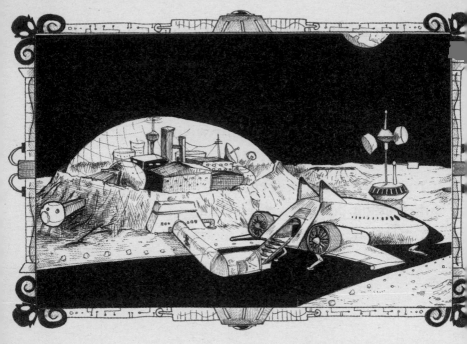

28

To the left of the moon base, you see a space shuttle standing outside a hangar.

If you wish to investigate the hangar, go to 4.
If you wish to investigate the shuttle, go to 33.

29

"How do you know this?" you ask.

Commander Peters smiles. "Because I am the alien!" In an instant, the commander transforms into an alien creature.

It grabs hold of your head. You struggle, but cannot break free of its deadly grip. You feel your mind slipping away as the creature takes over your body. You have been turned into an alien!

You have failed. If you wish to begin your mission again, go to 1.

30

You make your way to the briefing room. Professor Stevens is waiting for you.

He hands out the special equipment you will take. This includes life support systems, body armour, an energy pistol, special sat nav maps of the base and an emergency communication radio.

Then he points at two items. One is a huge gun and the other is a large backpack with a hand-held scanner. "A laser blaster and an alien life form detector," explains the professor.

You look at the size of the items and shake your head. "I won't be able to carry it all," you say. "I'll have to move quickly. I'll only take one of these."

If you want to take the laser gun go to 22.
If you want to take the ALF detector go to 14.

31

"Come out," you shout.

You gasp as a woman steps out of the shadows. "I'm Commander Peters," she says. "I thought you might be the alien, that's why I was hiding. We were attacked. I'm the only one left alive. It was terrible…"

If you wish to hear the commander's story, go to 9.

If you wish to switch on the ALF detector, go to 47.

32

You check the atmosphere in the moon base. There is little oxygen – you are glad you didn't remove your helmet.

You take out your com link device and bring up the sat nav map of the base. As you move through the corridors, there is no sign of any living thing – alien or human. Turning a corner, you come to a dead end with two doors.

If you wish to enter the control room, go to 24.
If you wish to enter the communications room, go to 45.

33

You make your way to the shuttle. A ladder leads up to an open door on the space craft. You climb up into the shuttle and head towards the cockpit. There is a light flashing on the communications panel. At that moment you glance out of the window and see something moving in the hangar.

If you wish to listen to the message on the communications panel, go to 11.
If you wish to explore the hangar, go to 4.

34

You press the button for the door. It opens and you step inside.

As the lights flicker on you see a figure moving

in the shadows near the oxygen tanks. You reach for your energy pistol.

If you wish to shoot at the figure, go to 27.

If you wish to order the figure to come out, go to 31.

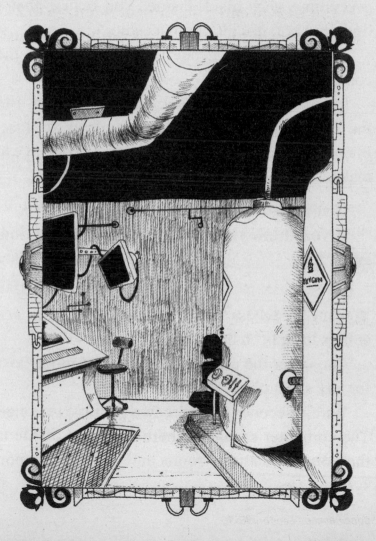

35

5...4...3...2...1... BLAST OFF!

You are thrust back into your seat by the g-force as the spaceship hurtles upwards.

Suddenly the Dart judders uncontrollably and everything goes black inside. You realise that a lightning bolt has hit the spaceship.

"Switch on emergency lights," you order the computer.

In seconds the emergency lights snap on. But the lightning has caused the controls to fuse. Flames flicker from the control panel. You have to make a quick decision.

If you wish to abort the mission, go to 10.

If you think you can deal with the situation, go to 2.

36

You try to access the logs, but all records and entries have been deleted.

You order the computer to scan the moon base for any signs of life.

Within seconds there are two positive readings. The computer speaks: "There are signs of life in the communications room and the life support systems area."

"Alien or human, and how many?" you ask.

"Unable to process," replies the computer. "There is not enough information to make a positive assessment."

You wonder where you should begin your search.

If you wish to investigate the signs of life in the communications room, go to 13.

If you wish to investigate the life support systems area, go to 21.

37

"What do I need to know?" you ask.

"There's a problem with the computer's auto flight control," says the professor. "You can't rely on it, especially if you were trying to fly through a meteor storm. If that does happen, then you must switch the controls to manual and fly the spaceship yourself."

"Thanks, I'll remember that. Is there anything else I need to know?"

"There is one more important point," says the professor. "When you want to land, set the computer's landing entry to 45 degrees. Anything higher than that will be fatal."

Now go to 5.

38

You point the weapon at the alien creature and signal it to move.

Suddenly, it leaps forward and heads towards the hangar door at incredible speed.

If you wish to shoot the alien, go to 17.
If you want to follow it, go to 26.

39

You switch on the ALF detector and point it towards the door. There is a moment's delay, then the screen flashes red – there is an alien life form in the communications room!

If you wish to enter the communications room, go to 45.
If you would prefer to search for the crew, go to 6.

40

Your angle of descent is too steep! The ship shakes uncontrollably and speeds up. The surface of the moon is getting nearer.

If you wish to change your angle of descent to 45 degrees, go to 25.
If you wish to continue on this angle, go to 16.

41

"This mission is too important to delay," you say. "I'll take the risk."

"It's your call," says the Launch Controller. "I just hope you've made the right decision."

You make your way to the pre-launch room and put on your space suit. Your chosen equipment is taken on board the Dart by the technicians.

You head out on to the launch pad where your Dart spaceship is waiting. Looking across the launch site, you notice dark clouds and lightning bolts flashing in the distance. This could be a dangerous take-off, you think, but you know that the mission is too important to delay.

You climb into the Dart, settle into your seat and tighten your safety harness.

"I'm all ready to go!" you say to the launch technicians and give a them thumbs-up.

The spaceship's door is shut behind you.

You make the final checks and get ready for the launch.

The countdown begins: 10...9...8...7...6...

Go to 35.

42

At the far side of the room, you see a pressure chamber. You know that this is used for treating astronauts who have suffered de-compression accidents. You run towards it.

The alien chases after you. You reach the chamber and quickly open the door.

If you wish to enter the pressure chamber, go to 3.

If you wish to shoot the alien, go to 17.

43

You arrive at the moon base entrance and open the airlock door. You step inside and close the outside lock. There is a hiss of air. You open the inner door.

You move slowly into the base. Moving down a metal corridor, you see that some of the utility pipes have been damaged. Steam pours out, causing your helmet to fog up and making it difficult to see properly.

If you wish to take off your space helmet, go to 7.

If you wish to keep your helmet on and search around, go to 32.

44

You switch on the auto flight as the meteors hurtle towards you. The ship is buffeted by the deadly storm.

A meteor hits the ship. The auto pilot isn't working! Another meteor hammers into the metal creating a huge hole.

The cabin is filled with wailing alarms and flashing lights. You try to switch off the auto pilot. It is too late! Another meteor hits.

The last thing you see is a flash of light as your spaceship is smashed apart.

If you want to begin the mission again, go back to 1.

45

You press the door button. As it opens, you gasp in horror. Standing before you is an alien creature! Before you can reach for your weapon, it grabs hold of you. You feel your mind slipping away as the creature takes over your body. You have been turned into an alien!

You have failed. If you wish to begin your mission again, go to 1.

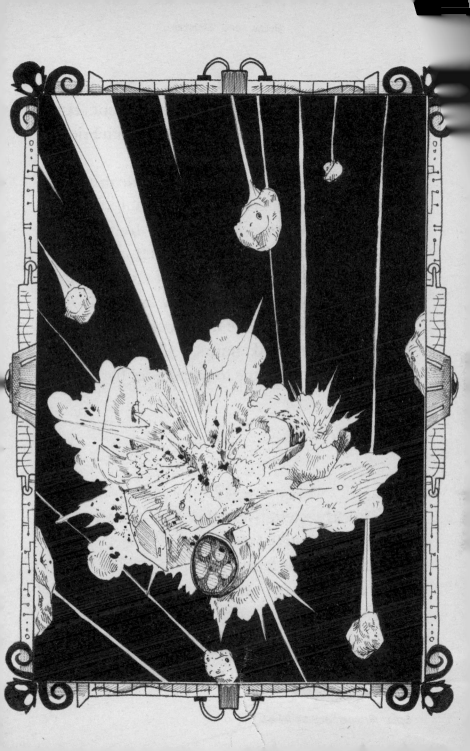

46

The director smiles. "I knew you wouldn't let me down. Read this," he says, handing you a briefing document.

You quickly flick through the e-book and take in the important points.

There are 12 men and women living on the moon base. Nothing has been heard from them, not even a distress signal. Recent images from satellites in Earth's orbit show no sign of an explosion or any damage to the base.

"You leave in six hours," says the director. "That will give you time to prepare for the mission. Good luck."

Now go to 30.

47

You quickly switch on the ALF detector. The screen immediately turns red.

"So you know what I am!"

You look up and see the commander transforming into an alien creature.

If you want to shoot the creature, go to 17.
If you wish to try to escape, go to 42.

48

You switch on your ALF detector and point it towards the oxygen tanks. The LCD screen flashes red – there is an alien life form hiding behind them! Slowly, you reach for your energy pistol.

If you wish to retreat to the moon base, go to 43.

If you wish to head towards the ALF, go to 23.

49

You switch the ship to manual flight.

You grip the controls tightly. The first meteor heads towards you and you flick the ship away from the deadly object.

Another meteor hurtles towards you. Again you steer the ship away. Your heart races as you guide the ship through the storm. Time after time, you are nearly hit, but you just manage to avoid the deadly meteors.

However, as the minutes pass, you realise that you are getting tired.

If you wish to abort th **go to 10.**

If you wish to carry on

50

You head back to the communications room and place the ALF detector against the door.

There are no signs of alien life, so you open the door. Inside are the crew of the moon base. They thank you for rescuing them. You order some of the crew to guard the pressure chamber.

Back in the control room, they tell you the story of how the alien took over Commander Peters and imprisoned them all.

Now that the alien is captured, the communications link to Earth is restored. You contact the director and inform him of your adventure.

"Well done," he says. "The Earth is safe for now! The alien cannot contact its home planet. The plan to invade Earth has failed! You are a real hero!"

QUIZ
SPACE RESCUE

YOU HAVE NOW COMPLETED YOUR MISSION. BUT CAN YOU RECALL THE KEY MOMENTS?
TAKE THIS QUIZ TO SEE HOW MUCH YOU CAN REMEMBER. THE ANSWERS ARE AT THE BACK OF THE BOOK. GOOD LUCK!

1 –   What are the initials of the space agency you work for?
a) NASA   b) UNSA
c) MENSA

2 –   What type of spaceship do you fly?
a)Arrow   b) Bullet
c) Dart

3 –   How many men and women live on the moon base?
a) 10   b) 12
c) 16

4 –   Who briefs you for your mission?
a) Professor Stevens
b) Professor Roberts
c) Professor Davis

5 – How do you survive the meteor storm?
a) fly around it   b) fly the ship manually
c) use the autopilot

6 – What is the correct angle of descent to land
on the moon?
a) 45 degrees   b) 75 degrees
c) 90 degrees

7 – What is the name of the commander of the
moonbase?
a) Commander Jones
b) Commander Stevens
c) Commander Peters

8 – What instrument tells you that an alien life
form is near?
a) an ELF detector   b) an OAF detector
c) an ALF detector

9 – The computer detects signs of life in the
communications room – and where else?
a) the life support area   b) the science lab
c) the shuttle hangar

10 – How does the alien overpower the moon
base crew?
a) It hypnotises them
b) by disguising itself as their commander
c) by shooting them with a stun gun

You are a member of Strike Force, a Special Forces operations squad. You have taken part in many dangerous missions throughout the world. Strike Force agents are only called in as a last resort and you are on standby 24 hours, 7 days a week.

As a senior member of the force, you are a martial arts and weapons expert. You also speak many languages. One morning you are training in the Strike Force base gym, when a soldier enters and salutes. "Nemesis wishes to see you straight away. It's a Code Black," he says. You thank the soldier and head towards the top secret Strike Force operations centre.

Nemesis is the codename for your boss, and Code Black is the highest mission level. Whatever task lies ahead for you, it is going to be very dangerous. You reach the operations centre and are directed to the secure briefing room. A guard opens the door and you enter. Sitting at a desk is your boss, Nemesis.

"We've got a situation," he says. "And we need you to deal with it."

Now turn to section 1.

1

Nemesis looks grimly at you. "We've no time to waste, so listen up. Victor Lokos, the President of the South American state of Amazonia is in Britain on an official state visit. His government has been very helpful in trying to destroy the drugs trade in his country."

You nod. "I was on a mission there last year – Operation Greenleaf. It was a difficult mission; we nearly lost several operatives due to some bad intelligence given by our contact, Manos. My team had to sort out the mess. We located and destroyed a drugs factory in the Amazon forest and arrested several gang members. No thanks to Manos."

Nemesis' voice is hard. "Operation Greenleaf didn't go down well with the drug barons. They swore revenge and it seems that they have lived up to their promise. We have a Code Black situation and I need you. However, it will mean that you will have to work with Manos again. I wouldn't ask you to do this if it wasn't important." You consider carefully. Manos nearly caused Operation Greenleaf to fail, but this sounds like an important mission.

If you decide that you don't want to work with Manos, go to 35.

If you agree to work with Manos, go to 12.

2

"We have to stop the van," you tell Manos.

"How will we do that?" he asks. You have to make a quick decision.

If you want the helicopter to force the van off the road, go to 44.

If you want to attempt to drop onto the roof of the van, go to 19.

If you decide to shoot at the van's tyres, go to 41.

3

You put your foot down on the accelerator and speed through the country lanes. The sporty SUV screeches around corners, narrowly missing other vehicles.

The sat phone rings again. It is Nemesis. "You're too late," he says. "The girl has been kidnapped. The President is furious. He doesn't want you anywhere near the operation to rescue his granddaughter. I'll send in another team. Return to base."

You have failed. If you wish to begin your mission again, turn to 1.

4

You sling the machine-gun over your shoulder and step to the door's edge.

"Ten metre drop, go!" you shout at Manos. He releases the winch brake and you leap out backwards. You plunge downwards for ten metres and then the rope yanks tight. You are now dangling above the roof of the van, travelling fast.

You glance ahead and see some electricity pylons. There are cables spanning the road. In less than thirty seconds you will hit them. You have to react immediately!

If you want to order Manos to winch you back up immediately, go to 20.

If you wish to shoot at the van, go to 26.

If you want to try to attach the tracking bug to the van's roof, go to 36.

5

As the van heads towards the helicopter, you shout at the pilot to fly higher.

He does so just in time. The roof of the van brushes the undercarriage of the helicopter as it accelerates down the road.

"Keep the van in sight," you order.

The helicopter and van chase along the road at high speed.

If you want to attempt to drop onto the roof of the van, go to 19.

If you decide to shoot at the van's tyres, go to 41.

6

"How do you know all this?" you ask.

"I have an informer in the gang," Manos replies. "His codename is Puma. He has told me that a kidnap attempt is going to happen very soon."

"And is this information reliable?" you ask.

"I would trust Puma with my life."

"It might not be your life that is on the line," you tell Manos. "It might be mine…"

Go to 18.

7

As you swing wildly on the rope, you shoot at the van, but miss your target.

The electricity cables are getting nearer. You signal Manos to winch you up.

Go to 17.

8

You order the helicopter pilot to slow down.

Eventually you reach the school and the helicopter lands. The other military units have already arrived, but they are too late. Several policemen are dead and the kidnappers have taken the girl. You radio Nemesis and tell him what has happened. He is furious. "You slowed down! What sort of agent are you! Don't bother coming back to base! You are finished in Strike Force, you coward!" Someone else will have to try and rescue the girl.

If you wish to start your mission again, go to 1.

9

"Manos is right," you say. "We should take the Strike Force helicopter. It's loaded with weapons and equipment, and ready for takeoff at five minutes notice."

Nemesis nods in agreement. "Very well. Get to the school and bring back the girl before the gang get to her. Your Code Black orders are not to return without her. Understood? Good luck."

Go to 46.

10

The van continues to speed along the country lanes. Although the helicopter pilot does his best, it is getting more difficult to follow it. It won't be long before it gets away.

If you want the helicopter to force the van off the road, go to 44.

If you want to attempt to drop onto the roof of the van, go to 19.

11

"Keep following the target," you tell the pilot. "But don't get too close, we want them to think they've lost us."

Using the tracking device, you follow the van for some time. Finally the van stops. You circle around before flying nearer. The van is parked in a disused industrial estate, outside a warehouse. You radio the location to Strike Force base. Nemesis tells you that other units are half an hour away. "That's too long," you say. "The gang are nervous – they could kill the girl and try to escape. We need to go in now and surprise them."

If you want to land and search on foot, go to 33.

If you want to search the warehouse using the helicopter's heat-detecting equipment, go to 37.

12

You realise that you have to trust Nemesis's judgement. "If you say it is important, I'll work with him."

"Thank you." Nemesis smiles and presses an intercom button. "Send Manos in." The door opens and Manos enters. "You two know each other," says Nemesis. You glare at Manos. He steps forward and holds out his hand.

If you wish to shake his hand, go to 25.
If you wish to ignore his greeting, go to 43.

13

Before you can ready your weapon and fire, you see a gun pointing at you.

A volley of shots ring out. Pain rips through your body and blackness engulfs you. Your failure has cost you your life.

If you wish to begin the mission again, go to 1.

14

You order the pilot to circle as the gang bundle the girl into their van. As they make their getaway, you tell the pilot to follow the van. You radio Nemesis and ask him to tell the other units to track the Strike Force helicopter.

The chase continues and it begins to get dark.

You switch on the helicopter's searchlight. The van speeds along country lanes and it gets harder to keep it in sight.

"What do you think we should do?" asks Manos.

If you wish to continue the chase, go to 10.

If you decide that you need to try to make the van stop, go to 2.

15

As you stand up, you see a man moving behind a stack of boxes, ten metres to your left. He obviously hasn't seen you.

You dive to the floor and crawl towards the boxes. You get nearer and nearer. As you are about to leap up and open fire, you hear a girl crying.

You realise that the granddaughter is also behind the boxes. You can't begin shooting, you might hit her.

You move quickly across the ground. In an instant you are behind the stack of boxes and you point your gun at the gang member.

He throws up his hands and cries out, "Don't shoot, I am Puma!"

If you want to ignore him and open fire, go to 13.

If you wish to listen to what he has to say, go to 34.

16

The lights of the van are blinding. "Stay here!" you order the pilot.

Just as it seems as though the van is going to crash into the helicopter, it swerves away. There is a terrible screeching noise as the van tips over and rolls towards the trees at the side of the road. You look on in horror as the van smashes into a tree and bursts into flames. You leap out of the helicopter, but it is too late, everyone in the van is dead. You have killed the President's granddaughter – you have failed.

If you wish to begin your mission again, go to 1.

17

Manos switches on the winch and you fly upwards.

The cables are almost upon you. The pilot pulls the helicopter up and misses them by centimetres, but for you it is too late. Dangling helplessly, you spin into the cables. Sparks light up the sky and you scream in agony as the deadly electricity brings your mission to an end.

If you wish to begin your adventure again, go back to 1.

18

You turn to Nemesis. "So what do you need me for?" you ask. "Surely it is a police job to protect the girl?"

"The President asked for you personally. He wants you to guard his granddaughter. He thinks highly of you because of the work you did on Operation Greenleaf. In the meantime, an armed police unit has been sent to the school to make sure she is safe until you arrive. Bring back the girl so we can protect her until we discover who the kidnappers are. Take Manos with you."

You are not happy about this. "Is that necessary?" you ask.

"Yes, and that's an order…" replies Nemesis.

If you agree to let Manos accompany you, go to 39.

If you want to disobey Nemesis's order, go to 49.

19

"I'm going to abseil down onto the roof. You operate the winch," you say to Manos.

You put on a harness and attach the winch rope to a metal clip. A gust of wind hits you in the face as you open the door. You tell the helicopter pilot to fly directly over the roof of the van. You put on your night-vision goggles. You reach into the Strike Force equipment box and pick up a magnetic tracking bug. But which weapon should you take?

If you decide to sling a machine-gun over your shoulder, go to 4.

If you would prefer to take a handgun, go to 28.

20

You order Manos to winch you back up.

The electricity cables get nearer and nearer as you are pulled upwards. The pilot pulls hard on the controls and the helicopter easily misses the cables. The helicopter swings around and you search below for the van.

You fly around in vain, looking for the van. You have lost it. You radio Nemesis.

He is furious. "I'll let the other units deal with this. Return to base."

You have failed. If you wish to begin again, go to 1.

21

"You're worrying too much," you tell Manos. "The kidnappers won't strike yet. We'll take the SUV."

"Keep in contact on your journey and good luck," says Nemesis.

You leave the room with Manos and head over to the Strike Force vehicle compound. The SUV is loaded with Strike Force weapons and equipment.

"I'll drive, you get in and check the weapons," you tell Manos. He does so. You programme the sat nav system and set off.

You have been driving for 15 minutes, when your sat phone rings. It is Nemesis. "We have reports of armed attackers at the school. You need to get there immediately!"

If you wish to drive as fast as possible to the school, go to 3.

If you wish to return to the base and take the helicopter, go to 31.

22

You pick up Helena and carefully make your way back with Puma to Manos.

You tell Puma to help Manos outside and radio your helicopter to come and pick you up. Seconds later, you see several other helicopters flying low. Ropes are flung out and squads of soldiers abseil down and rush towards the warehouse. You smile, knowing that the surviving members of the gang will soon be dealt with.

You and Puma lift Helena and Manos into the helicopter before climbing in yourselves. "Let's go home," you tell the pilot.

Go to 50.

23

You order the pilot to increase speed. Soon the helicopter is hovering over the school.

You radio Nemesis and he tells you that there are reports of police casualties. The gang have already seized the President's granddaughter and are heading towards their escape vehicle at the rear of the school.

You pick up your machine-gun and order the pilot to fly to the rear of the school.

The pilot obeys and within seconds you spot a group of men heading towards a van. You can see that they are dragging a young girl with them. It must be the granddaughter, you think.

Police are following, but not firing. What should you do?

If you choose to fly in and shoot at the gang members, go to 38.

If you decide to land the helicopter near the escape vehicle, go to 33.

If you would rather let the gang get into their van and follow it in the helicopter, go to 14.

24

You take a combat knife from your belt and cut the rope.

You drop onto the van's roof with a thump. The van accelerates forward and you nearly slide off. Somehow you manage to keep your balance and attach the tracking bug to the roof. Having done what you needed to do, you brace yourself and leap off the roof. You hit the road and roll over and over.

Go to 27.

25

For the sake of the mission, you shake Manos's hand.

"I am sorry for what happened in Operation Greenleaf," Manos says. "I give you my word that I will make no mistakes this time."

You are still wary of Manos, but accept his apology. "Very well. So what is this all about?" you ask.

Manos hands you a file marked 'ULTRA TOP SECRET". You open it and see a picture of a young girl. Manos begins his briefing.

"This is Helena Lokos, the President's granddaughter. For the past year she has secretly been a pupil in Britain at a boarding school called Bearham Park. No one knows her true identity. However, on his visit to Britain, the President said he wanted to visit Helena. This has led to a security breach. Helena's true identity and her location are now in the open. I have had information that the drug barons intend to kidnap her. They will then kill her if the President doesn't release all gang members captured in Operation Greenleaf." You need to know more information about the mission.

Who should you ask?

If you wish to direct your questions to Nemesis, go to 18.

If you wish to ask Manos, go to 6.

26

You try to take the machine-gun from your shoulder, but on the swinging rope you struggle to reach it. You're taking too long! Through your night-vision goggles you see a figure shooting at you from the van. Bullets rip into you. Your lifeless body hangs from the rope.

You have failed completely. If you wish to start again, turn back to 1.

27

The van speeds away as you stand up and brush yourself down. You speak into your radio. "Pick me up."

Minutes later the helicopter has landed and you climb inside. "Well done," says Manos. You switch on the tracking system and breathe a sigh of relief. The tracker is working. What is your plan of action?

If you wish to return to base and let other units deal with the situation, go to 45.

If you decide to follow the van, go to 11.

28

You pick up the handgun and step to the door's edge.

"Ten metre drop, go!" you tell Manos. He releases the winch brake and you leap out backwards. You plunge downwards for ten metres and then the rope yanks tight. You are now dangling above the roof of the van, travelling fast. You glance ahead and see some electricity pylons. There are cables spanning the road. In less than thirty seconds you will hit them. You have to react immediately!

If you want to try to attach the tracking bug, go to 36.

If you want to order Manos to winch you back up immediately, go to 20.

If you wish to stay where you are and shoot at the van, go to 7.

29

"Let me see the injury."

As you bend forward, Manos brings his gun up and points it at you. You stare in horror and brace yourself for the impact. He pulls the trigger and a stream of bullets fly over your shoulder. There is a cry from behind you and you spin around to see a gang member falling to the floor.

You realise that Manos has saved your life. "Thanks," you say.

"See, I can be trusted," replies Manos, "Now leave me and get the girl!"

Go to 15.

30

"Lower me five metres," you shout into your radio.

Manos obeys and you drop onto the roof of the van with a thump. As you do, the van accelerates forward. You fix the tracking bug onto the roof of the van. The cables are getting closer. How will you get off the roof?

If you decide to cut your rope, go to 40.

If you want to order Manos to winch you back up, go to 17.

31

You swing on the wheel of the car and spin it around. You put your foot down on the accelerator and speed along the country lanes, knowing that there is no time to lose.

The car screeches around corners, narrowly missing other vehicles. You radio ahead and tell them to get the helicopter ready for immediate takeoff.

Your expert driving gets you back to the base in record time. You slide the car to a halt, jump out and head to the Strike Force helicopter. Manos follows.

Go to 46.

32

You take aim and let go of the tracking bug.

However, as you do so, the van accelerates forward. The bug drops down, hits the side of the roof and bounces onto the ground.

You curse loudly. There is no time to try to place another tracker.

Go to 20.

33

You order the pilot to land the helicopter near the gang's van.

As he does so, the gang open fire. Moving so slowly, the helicopter is a sitting target! You return fire and shout, "Pull away!"

It is too late. A stream of bullets rips through the helicopter. You feel a searing pain in your chest and drop to the floor. You have paid the ultimate price.

If you wish to begin your mission again, return to 1.

34

"Are you Manos's contact?" you ask.

"Yes," he answers and slowly moves aside to reveal the President's granddaughter. "I moved her away from the rest of the gang when your attack began. We need to get her away from the others that are left. They will surely kill her as a punishment." You nod in agreement and hold out your hand.

"Come with me, Helena. You're going to be safe." Still trembling, she takes hold of your hand.

Go to 22.

35

"I'm afraid I don't want to work with him," you say. "I can't trust him."

Nemesis is not impressed. "I could order you to do this. And if you refuse…"

What should you do?

If you agree to work with Manos, go to 12.
If you still don't want to, go to 49.

36

You take the tracking bug from your pocket and flick the switch to activate it.

It is magnetic and will stick to the roof. You are five metres above the roof and the cables are getting nearer. How will you attach the tracking bug to the roof?

If you want to drop it onto the roof and hope it sticks, go to 32.

If you wish to order Manos to lower you onto the roof, and then attach it, go to 30.

If you wish to cut your rope and drop onto the roof, go to 24.

37

You order the pilot to fly around, whilst you check out the warehouse. The heat-detecting equipment helps you to pinpoint the gang. They are on the ground floor, near the front of the building.

You look carefully at the incoming visuals. You can make out six figures. You guess that one of these must be the President's granddaughter, leaving five gang members.

You smile. These are the sort of odds you like! How should you attack the warehouse?

If you wish to make a full-frontal attack, go to 33.

If you wish to attack the rear of the building, go to 48.

38

You unclip the safety catch on your machine-gun. As you take aim, Manos grabs hold of your arm.

"You can't risk such a shot!" he hisses. "You might hit the girl!"

You pause. Is Manos right? Should you choose another option?

If you wish to ignore Manos, go to 47.

If you decide to land the helicopter near the escape vehicle, go to 33.

If you would rather let the gang get into their van and follow it in the helicopter, go to 14.

39

"Very well," you say. "How far is the school from here?"

"Two hours by road," says Nemesis. "You could take a Strike Force SUV."

"Two hours is a long time," says Manos. "We could be too late."

If you agree with Manos, go to 9.
If you disagree with him, go to 21.

40

You take a knife from your belt and cut your rope. The helicopter pulls away.

Having done what you needed to do, you brace yourself and leap off the roof. You hit the road and roll over and over.

Go to 27.

41

You open the helicopter's door.

You pick up your gun, take aim at the van's tyres and pull the trigger. Your gun kicks back and a stream of bullets light up the sky. The van driver swerves in order to avoid the attack as you continue to fire at the vehicle.

Suddenly, the tyres of the van burst. The vehicle lurches across the road. You watch in horror as it spins wildly across the road and hits a tree. There is an explosion and the van is engulfed in flames.

"You fool!" cries Manos. "You've killed the President's granddaughter."

You have failed in you mission. If you wish to begin again, go to 1.

42

You throw a stun grenade. The air is full of noise and smoke. You move forward carefully, looking for the girl.

Suddenly there is a burst of fire from your right and Manos is hit. You spin round and return fire. The man who shot Manos drops to the ground.

You rush to Manos and kneel over him. "I'm all right," he says. "It's just my leg. You go on."

If you want to deal with Manos's injury, go to 29.

If you want to continue your hunt for the girl, go to 15.

43

You stand facing Manos. "Your bad intelligence nearly cost my team's lives," you say.

"I am sorry you feel like that," replies Manos. "I can assure you I was acting in good faith. Will you forgive me?" You remain silent.

"We need his help, so I am ordering you to accept his apology," says Nemesis.

If you wish to obey Nemesis, go to 25.
If you don't, go to 49.

44

You tell the pilot to fly over the van. He accelerates past the vehicle at top speed.

You are four hundred metres ahead of the van, when you tell him to turn the helicopter round and hover just above the road. He does so. The van's headlights shine brightly as it speeds towards you. It is not slowing down!

If you wish to shoot at the van, go to 41.

If you decide to order the pilot to fly higher, go to 5.

If you decide to keep the helicopter in position, go to 16.

45

You return to the Strike Force base and head to the operations centre. Nemesis is amazed to see you.

"Where is the girl?" he asks. You tell him what happened. He is furious. "I gave you a Code Black order not to return without her!" You try to explain, but he will not listen to you. "But the girl is not here!" he growls.

Go to 49.

46

You climb into the helicopter, put on your communication device and order the pilot to head to the school at top speed.

As the helicopter skims over the treetops, you radio Nemesis for an update. He tells you that the gang have seized the girl and are currently engaged in a shoot-out with armed police. Other military units have been sent to the school, but will not reach it before you do.

If you decide to wait for these units to arrive, go to 8.

If you wish to get to the school as quickly as possible, go to 23.

47

You shrug away Manos's protests and pull the trigger. Bullets rain down on the gang. They return fire. As the battle continues, you see the girl drop to the floor. You've hit her!

"You fool!" screams Manos. "What have you done?" The gang continues to fire at the helicopter. It takes a direct hit to the rotors and you plunge to the ground.

You have failed completely. If you wish to start again, turn back to 1.

48

You tell the pilot to land the helicopter away from the warehouse. As he does, you and Manos arm yourselves and put on gas masks and helmets.

The helicopter comes to a halt and you tell the pilot to begin a frontal attack on the warehouse on your command. You leap out with Manos and head for the rear of the warehouse. There is a shutter door, which is locked. You place an explosive device against it and then use your radio to order the helicopter pilot to make an attack on the front of the building. You hear the helicopter zooming in, guns blazing. You hit the detonator and the door explodes. You rush in.

If you decide to throw stun grenades, go to 42.

If you wish to begin shooting, go to 13.

49

"No," you say, grimly.

"Then get out!" shouts Nemesis. "As a member of Strike Force, you know that disobeying an order means it is the end of your career!" You leave. Your career in Strike Force is over.

If you wish to begin the adventure again, return to 1.

50

Some days later you are called into the Strike Force operations centre. Nemesis sits at his desk.

"What mission is it now?" you ask.

"Nothing for the moment. There's someone who wanted to see you."

The door opens and Manos limps in. You nod towards his leg. "Just a scratch," he smiles. "My president wishes to thank you for the great service you did."

"Just doing my job," you reply. "While there are bad people out there, Strike Force has to be ready to deal with them."

He nods. "Puma and I are moving into other fields of intelligence, but perhaps we will meet again."

"Perhaps we will," you say. "I look forward to it." You hold out your hand. He takes it and gives you a firm handshake.

"Thank you again, you are a real hero!"

QUIZ
STRIKE FORCE

YOU HAVE NOW COMPLETED YOUR MISSION. BUT CAN YOU RECALL THE KEY MOMENTS?
TAKE THIS QUIZ TO SEE HOW MUCH YOU CAN REMEMBER. THE ANSWERS ARE AT THE BACK OF THE BOOK. GOOD LUCK!

1 – What is your boss's codename?
   a) Narcissus   b) Nubia
   c) Nemesis

2 – What is the code colour for the highest mission level?
   a) Code Black   b) Code Red
   c) Code Yellow

3 – What was the codename of your previous mission in Amazonia?
   a) Operation Greenleaf
   b) Operation Tealeaf
   c) Operation Greenwood

4 – Which Agent failed you on that mission?
   a) Agent Nino   b) Agent Manos
   c) Agent Carlos

5 – What is the name of the President of Amazonia?
a) President Artos   b) President Markos
c) President Lokos

6 – What is the name of the President's granddaughter?
a) Hannah   b) Helena
c) Harriet

7 – Where does she go to school?
a) Bearham Park   b) Deerham House
c) Foxton Hall

8 – What is the codename of the informer among the kidnappers?
a) Cougar   b) Puma
c) Panther

9 – Where is your fellow agent shot during the attack on the kidnappers' base?
a) in the leg   b) in the shoulder
c) in the arm

10 - How do you escape from the gang's hideout?
a) by jeep   b) by helicopter
c) by van

TOMB RUNNER

You are one of the world's leading treasure hunters. Your talent for archaeology is only matched by your skills in martial arts and languages. You have travelled the world searching for, and discovering, priceless treasures and artefacts. Many of these adventures have been dangerous, but you have always succeeded in bringing back the archaeological treasures you set out to find. This has made you – and the charities you support – very rich.

In your latest quest you are trying to discover the hiding place of Blackbeard the Pirate's treasure. You are in your library, studying an antique map, when your butler enters. He coughs.

"What is it, Peters?" you ask.

"I'm sorry to disturb you," he replies, "but there is a gentleman in the lobby. He wishes to see you. He says it is very important. Here is his card."

"Interesting," you say. "J P Greenback – he's an American who has made a fortune in oil. He's used his money to put together one of the world's greatest collections of ancient objects. What does he want, I wonder? Show him in Peters."

Now turn to section 1.

1

A few moments later, the library door opens and Peters shows in J P Greenback Jnr.

"Howdee," he says, shaking your hand. "JP's my name. It is a pleasure and a privilege to meet such a famous adventurer." He glances around your library. "Quite a collection, you have here."

"I have heard that yours is a greater one," you reply. "I believe you have a lot of money to spend on it."

"Now that is very true!" Greenback smiles. "I cannot deny that I do have a lot of money, probably more money than I really need. But money can't buy you everything. However, I believe it will help me to buy your services."

If are offended by Greenback's words, go to 20.

If you want to know how much Greenback wishes to offer, go to 49.

2

Before Sükh can react, you grab hold of his arm and stun him with a karate chop.

He staggers to his knees and drops the gun on the floor.

You have to make an immediate decision. Should you reach for the gun or use your martial arts skills to defeat Sükh?

If you want to pick up the gun, go to 28.

If you decide to use your fighting skills, go to 42.

3

You drive slowly towards the ravine and edge the jeep onto the bridge. It creaks and rocks violently. You drive further onto the bridge.

Suddenly there is a loud crack as the ropes begin to snap. You have to make an immediate decision.

If you want to try and drive across the bridge at speed, go to 24.

If you decide to grab your bag and get out of the jeep, go to 45.

4

Greenback suddenly screams.

The figure of a ghostly warrior emerges from the tomb, takes the sword out of his hand, and plunges it into his chest. More ghostly warriors follow, armed with swords.

As you look on in horror at the scene, the leader of the Guardians places his hand on your shoulder.

"If you are of true heart, stay still," he says.

If you want to try and run away, go to 40.

If you decide to do as the leader of the Guardians says, go to 25.

5

Over the next day, you research more about Genghis Khan.

He was originally called Temüjin, and only took the name of Genghis Khan when he defeated his enemies and was made ruler of all the Mongols. Your research backs up Greenback's story about the location of the monastery in a hidden valley in Mongolia.

You try and find the hidden valley using satellite imagery on your computer. However, no matter what you do, you cannot get a clear picture of the location.

Very strange, you think, I wonder what is causing that…

Now go to 15.

6

The room is lined with wooden shelves on which lie many ancient manuscripts and maps. You realise that you have found the monastery's library. On the far wall of the room is a large prayer wheel.

If you wish to search for the manuscript that reveals the location of the tomb, go to 23.

If you wish to spin the prayer wheel, go to 37.

7

You wake up in a cold stone cell. Your hands and legs are chained to a wall. Several men dressed in black robes are standing over you.

"Who are you?" you ask.

One of the men steps forward. "We are the Guardians of the Tomb of Genghis Khan. We are sworn to keep it secret from the outside world."

You feel sick in your stomach. "What are you going to do with me?"

"Nothing. Quite literally."

They leave the cell, slamming the heavy wooden door shut and plunging you into darkness. You realise that you will never get out alive…

You have failed in your quest. If you wish to begin again, turn back to 1.

8

You hold up the glow stick, but it has no effect – the creature moves towards you. You struggle to free yourself from its web, but it is useless. You are stuck fast!

The creature's deadly jaws open and then snap shut, cutting off your cries forever.

You have failed. If you wish to try again, go back to 1.

9

"Tell me more," you say.

"Through a series of informants, I have discovered that there is a manuscript hidden in the library of a Buddhist monastery which tells exactly where the tomb is located. This monastery is in a secret valley in Northern Mongolia."

"If you know so much, why do you need me?" you ask. "Just go yourself."

Greenback shakes his head. "I do not wish to bring attention to the quest. The Mongolian authorities take a dim view of people trying to discover the location of the tomb and removing what treasures may lie within it. You have a reputation for secrecy and getting the job done. I need you…"

If you wish to take up this adventure, go to 32.

If you would prefer to stick to trying to discover Blackbeard's treasure, go to 43.

10

"You've been searching for the tomb of Genghis Khan, you should open the one that bears his name," you reply.

Greenback orders his men to open the tomb. They use crowbars to force off the lid and stand back to allow Greenback to look into the tomb.

He peers in, "There is no body in here. Just this." He pulls out a rusty sword.

"The sword of the Khan," says the leader of the Guardians of the Tomb. "To keep good men true and reward evil men with their just deserts."

Go to 4.

11

You continue along the ledge and soon reach the tunnel at the far side of the cavern.

You light another glow stick and make your way through the dark passage. After some time you see light ahead of you. You run towards it and step out into a huge valley, surrounded by snow-topped mountains. In the distance you see a monastery.

"This must be the hidden valley!" you mutter. "Now to find the manuscript!"

If you want to walk into the monastery, go to 41.

If you want to try and enter the monastery without being seen, go to 18.

12

You dive into the jeep, pulling the dead Sükh in with you to act as a shield. Bullets shatter the side window and door.

Frantically, you search through Sükh's pockets and find the keys to the jeep.

If you want to try to drive away immediately, go to 22.

If you want to wait for the firing to stop, go to 46.

13

You dive into the icy cold water and begin swimming towards the tunnel.

Suddenly the water churns up around you. Thousands of tiny carnivorous fish surround you and begin biting at you. You thrash about, trying to get away, but it is helpless – there are too many of them. Bit by bit they eat at your flesh. Your blood mixes with the black water and you sink into the cold depths.

You have failed. If you wish to begin again, turn back to 1.

14

Smiling, you walk up to the guards with your hands held out. "Excuse me, I seem to be lost," you say.

The guards looked confused at your sudden appearance. Before they can react you attack, knocking them unconscious.

Stepping over their bodies, you enter the room. It is empty except for a large prayer wheel standing in the middle of the room.

You hear a noise in the corridor.

If you want to leave the room, go to 28.

If you wish to spin the prayer wheel, go to 37.

15

Two days later, you set off for Mongolia. After a comfortable flight, you arrive at Chinggis Khan, the international airport for Ulan Bator.

You make your way to arrivals and are approached by a man.

"Welcome to Mongolia," he says. "I am Sükh, your guide. Please follow me to your vehicle."

If you wish to follow Sükh, go to 48.

If you don't trust him, go to 36.

16

You leave the room and pass by groups of captured Guardians being watched over by Greenback's men.

Using the manuscript's directions, Greenback and some of his group take you and the leader of the Guardians of the Tomb down into the cellars of the monastery.

Greenback orders the Guardians' leader to tell him where the entrance to the chamber is. To your surprise he points to a trapdoor in the floor. One of Greenback's men lifts it up.

If you want to take this opportunity to try to escape, go to 46.

If you want to go into the chamber, go to 44.

17

You pack your bag with essential supplies: the sat phone, climbing ropes, glow sticks and your pistol and ammunition. You leave the jeep and step out onto the bridge. The river rages far below and you see sharp rocks jutting upwards.

Just as you reach the halfway point, the bridge begins to shake violently. You look behind you and see a figure using a curved sword to chop at the ropes from which the wooden roadway hangs!

Before you can reach for your gun, the bridge begins to break up.

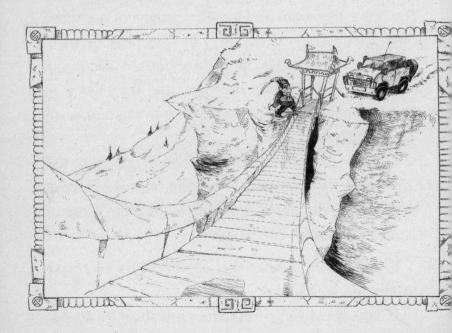

If you want to sprint for the other side of the bridge, go to 24.

If you decide to wrap your arms around the bridge ropes and hang on, go to 45.

18

You decide to move around the edge of the valley before making your way towards the rear of the monastery.

Soon you are standing at the foot of the monastery wall.

Using a grappling rope from your pack, you climb up the wall and drop silently into the monastery.

With your gun out, you make your way along an open corridor that has several doors leading off it.

Suddenly there is a sound of voices coming towards you. Two guards dressed in black robes appear. What should you do?

If you want to find somewhere to hide, go to 31.

If you want to order them to take you to their leader, go to 26.

If you want to run away from the guards, go to 28.

19

"You should open the one that says 'Temüjin'," you reply. "That was Genghis Khan's real name."

Greenback orders his men to open the tomb. They use crowbars to force off the lid and stand back to allow Greenback to look into the tomb.

He peers in, "I don't believe this," he cries out. They are the last words he utters…

Go to 40.

20

"Mr Greenback," you say angrily. "I do not care for your manner. I am offended by what you imply. You will apologise or I will ask Peters to show you the door."

Greenback looks embarrassed. "I am sorry, I didn't mean to annoy you. It is just my way. Please accept my apology."

You nod. "I do. Now what brings you here?"

"I have an adventure for you. However, it is dangerous – it will test you to your limits. But I will pay you handsomely if you choose to undertake it."

If you are more interested in the adventure than the money, go to 38.

If you are more interested in what you will be paid, go to 49.

21

The creature gets closer and you reach for your gun.

As the spider's deadly jaws open you aim your weapon into the blackness of its mouth and pull the trigger again and again. Bullets tear into its body and a nightmarish scream echoes around the cavern.

The spider falls into the water, which bubbles up into a churning whirlpool, before returning to a black stillness.

Breathing deeply, you free yourself from the web.

If you wish to continue making your way along the ledge, go to 11.

If you would now prefer to swim across to the tunnel, go to 13.

22

You push Sükh's body out of the vehicle. With bullets ripping into the bodywork, you start up the jeep, slam your foot onto the accelerator and speed off.

Soon you are out of range. Thankful for your escape, you drive on for some time. Once you have left Ulan Bator far behind you pull off the road to check the jeep.

It is full of the equipment you ordered – food, water, clothes, ropes, glow sticks... and an automatic pistol. You also check your bag to see whether the satellite phone is damaged. Luckily it isn't. You decide to head for the hidden valley.

Go to 39.

23

You begin to search through the manuscripts for the one that contains the location of the tomb. However, there are hundreds of them and you realise that this will take far too long: you will need someone to tell you where the manuscript is.

If you want to leave the library to look for help, go to 47.

If you think spinning the prayer wheel will help, go to 37.

24

You have made a fatal mistake! The ropes snap and you plunge down into the ravine, screaming with fear and the knowledge that you are about to die.

You have failed in your quest. If you wish to begin again, turn back to 1.

25

You remain still. Greenback's men panic and begin shooting, but their bullets have no effect on the ghostly warriors. Soon Greenback's men are all dead and the ghosts vanish again.

"Who were those beings?" you ask. "And why am I still alive?"

The leader of the Guardians turns to you. "They are the ghosts of the Mongol warriors. Forever sworn to protect their leader, Genghis Khan, and to bring death to all evil men. The Sword summoned them from their graves. It is as well that you are not a follower of he who took the sword: otherwise, you would be dead. Why did you choose to open that tomb?" he asks.

"I remembered the line in the manuscript," you reply. "The sword that conquered the world will bring destruction to evil men. I thought that Genghis Khan would be buried with the name he began with – Temujin."

The leader nods. "You chose wisely. But now you have another choice to make. Do you wish to open Temujin's tomb and see what treasures lie there?"

You think of the money that you could make telling the world about the tomb.

If you wish to open the tomb, go to 33.
If you don't, go to 50.

26

You point your gun at the guards. "Take me to the head of this monastery," you repeat.

In reply, one of the guards kicks the gun from your hand and launches a fearsome attack. You fight back, using all your martial arts skills. You manage to knock out one of the guards, but the other one catches you with a stunning high kick to your head. You drop to the floor, unconscious.

Go to 7.

27

"Mr Greenback, Mongolia is a vast country – thousands of people have searched in vain for the tomb. It will never be found. I am far too busy to chase a fantasy."

Greenback shakes his head. "It is no fantasy, I am sure of the location of the tomb. And if you do not find it, I will still pay you."

If you wish to hear more about the location of the tomb, go to 9.

If you want to ask about what you will be paid, go to 49.

If you are not interested in the quest, go to 43.

28

As you move, you feel a searing pain at the base of your neck. You drop to the floor, unconscious.

Go to 7.

29

"How did you get here?" you ask Greenback.

"The satellite phone I gave you has a tracking device in it," he replies. "My men and I have been following you from the moment you landed. I needed you to provide a distraction for these people."

He pushes forward a bald-headed man dressed in robes. "This is the head of this monastery and leader of the Guardians of the Tomb. My men have taken over the monastery and thanks to you, we will soon find the tomb of Genghis Khan and its treasure. I hope you won't refuse my invitation to join me?"

If you want to reach for your gun and shoot Greenback, go to 46.

If you agree to go along with Greenback, go to 16.

If you refuse to help Greenback, go to 34.

30

You climb the rope nearest the opening. However, this causes it to fray even more. Just as it is about to snap, you throw yourself to the side and grab hold of the bottom lip of the opening. Straining with all your might, you pull yourself into it.

Once you have recovered your breath, you reach into your bag, take out a glow stick and activate it. You head into the opening and realise that it leads into a tunnel. You walk on carefully and eventually arrive at a huge cavern with a lake. Lighting another glow stick, you can just make out a small ledge running around the lake which leads to another tunnel on the far side.

If you want to balance on the ledge around the side of the lake, go to 35.

If you want to swim across the lake to the tunnel, go to 13.

31

You open one of the doors on the corridor and quickly slip inside.

You wait at the door, listening carefully. You hear the guards pass by. What should you do now?

If you wish to explore this room, go to 6.

If you wish to leave the room, go to 47.

32

"I'm interested," you say. "Tell me more."

Greenback smiles. "The monastery is in a secret valley in the Khentii mountains, north-east of the Mongolian capital, Ulan Bator.

"You'll travel there and find the manuscript. If you can decode it, you should discover the location of the tomb. When you do, I want to know immediately and I will join you as soon as I can." He reaches into a bag and hands over a satellite phone. "Use this. It will scramble the message. I don't trust normal communication. Other people might be listening."

You wonder who the 'others' might be, but say nothing.

"In the meantime, I will make travel arrangements. A guide will meet you at the airport. His name is Jamuka. He will supply you with all your equipment."

Over the next hour you give Greenback a list of your requirements. Finally, he shakes your hand. "Hopefully, I will see you when you have discovered the tomb of Genghis Khan." Peters shows him to the door.

If you wish to find out more about Genghis Khan, go to 5.

If you wish to get on with your adventure, go to 15.

33

"I would love to," you reply.

"Then you are only a thief after all," replies the leader.

The air is once again filled with ghostly warriors, all with their weapons ready. One ghoulish figure speeds toward you. You scream and scream as its sword hacks at your body...

You failed the final test. If you wish to begin again, go back to 1.

34

"I'm not helping you any more," you say.

"Very well," replies Greenback, "I don't need you anymore."

The last sight you see is Greenbacks' men raising their weapons. The last sound you hear is the crack of the bullets heading towards your body...

Your adventure is over. If you wish to begin again, go to 1.

35

You hold the glow stick in your teeth, and begin to balance around on the narrow ledge.

As you move across, you feel a sticky, hair-like substance brush against your face. You continue on, but the strands become thicker and stickier, pulling at your body and entangling you.

As you try to struggle through, there is a blood curdling noise above you. You look up and your blood turns cold – it is a monstrous spider, heading towards you. You have wandered into its web!

If you want to escape by diving into the water, go to 13.

If you want to attack the spider, go to 21.

If you want to use the glow stick to frighten it off, go to 8.

36

"Where is Jamuka?" you ask.

Sükh shakes his head. "He has met with an accident. I am his replacement. Do not worry, I have all your equipment. It is in a jeep in the car park."

If you decide to follow Sükh, go to 48.

If you don't wish to follow him, go to 28.

37

You spin the prayer wheel. To your amazement a secret door opens in the wall.

You light a glow stick and enter a small room. There is a table on which lies an ancient manuscript. You begin to read it and realise that it is the manuscript that you have been searching for!

You continue to read through the document, translating it as you go. It tells you that the tomb you are looking for is located in a chamber beneath the monastery.

You finish reading the manuscript but are puzzled by one of the lines.

You read it out loud: "The sword that conquered the world will bring destruction to evil men." You wonder what it means.

Picking up the manuscript, you turn to leave the room, but a familiar voice makes you gasp and stop dead in your tracks.

"Well done! First you found the valley and now the manuscript. Now all we have to find is the tomb!"

You stare in amazement. Standing at the door is J P Greenback with a group of armed men!

Go to 29.

38

"As you can see, I am not poor," you say. "I am more interested in adventure."

"I am glad to hear it," replies Greenback. "Then I will tell you why I have come here. I am sure you know about the legend of the tomb of Genghis Khan?"

In reply, you reach into a drawer and pull out a large map. You place it on your desk and unfurl it.

You point at the map. "Genghis Khan founded the Mongol Empire in the thirteenth century. He was a great warrior and united the tribes of Central Asia. He died in 1227 and was buried somewhere in Mongolia. His tomb has never been found, although many people have searched for it… and usually ended up dead," you add.

"You know your history", says Greenback.

You shake your head and smile. "The legend of the tomb is just a story. No one will ever find it."

"Don't be so sure," Greenback replies. "I have obtained information about its location."

If you wish to hear more, go to 9.

If you think Greenback is wasting your time, go to 27.

39

You program your sat nav with the location of the hidden valley and begin your drive across the Mongolian plains.

Hours later, the terrain becomes more mountainous. Following your sat nav, you drive up a dirt track and eventually arrive at a deep ravine. There is a wooden bridge spanning the gap. You check on the sat nav – there is no way around. You will have to cross the bridge.

You assess the situation – the bridge is wide enough for the jeep, but will it take the weight?

If you decide to drive across, go to 3.

If you decide to leave the jeep and travel on foot, go to 17.

40

The chamber fills with hundreds of armed ghostly figures pouring out of the tomb.

Your mind suddenly realises who they are – the ghosts of the Mongol warriors, protecting their leader, Genghis Khan, and bringing death to all intruders.

Your last sight is of a ghostly sword plunging into your body and your very real blood pouring onto the floor.

Your adventure is over. If you wish to begin again, go to 1.

41

You make your way to the monastery entrance. You are stopped at the gate by two guards dressed in dark robes.

You bow and in perfect Mongolian say, "I would like to speak to the head of your monastery."

One of the guards shakes his head. "Go away stranger. You should not be here."

If you want to try to find a different way into the monastery, go to 28.

If you decide to threaten them with your gun, go to 26.

42

You leap at Sükh and hold his head in a chinlock. "Where is Jamuka and who are you working for?" you demand. "Tell me or I will break your neck."

"Let me go and I will tell you," gasps Sükh.

You release him a little, still keeping a firm grip on him. But before he can say anything you hear a gunshot. He slumps forward, dead. Blood seeps from his forehead.

More shots ring out, hitting the ground around you. You have to get out of this situation!

If you choose to jump into the jeep, go to 12.

If you want to run back to the airport building, go to 28.

43

You shake your head. "I am sorry, I am not interested in this fantasy. I have more real treasures to seek."

Peters shows Mr Greenback to the door.

Your adventure is over before it began. If you would like to start again, return to 1.

44

Greenback and his men take you and the Leader of the Guardians into the chamber. It is lit up by flaming torches. In the centre of the chamber are two stone tombs.

Greenback inspects them and calls you over. "You're the expert," he says, "why are there two tombs?"

You translate the inscriptions. "The one on the left says 'Here lies Temüjin', the one on the right says, 'Here lies Genghis Khan – the conquering sword.' I don't know what that means," you tell Greenback.

"Which one should we open first?" he asks. You recall the line in the manuscript that puzzled you: 'The sword that conquered the world will bring destruction to evil men.'

If you think you should open the tomb that says 'Temüjin', go to 19.

If you think you should open the one that says 'Genghis Khan', go to 10.

If you refuse to have anything more to do with Greenback, go to 34.

45

You leap for the rope that supports the bridge and wrap your arm tightly around it. Seconds later the bridge gives way, sending you hurtling towards the opposite cliff face.

You crash into the rock wall but manage to hold on. Swinging on the rope, you look around you. Below you, the river rages, but to your left there seems to be a small opening in the cliff.

The bridge judders again – the ropes above you are beginning to fray. You have to get out of here quickly!

If you want to climb up and out of the ravine, go to 24.

If you wish to try to reach the opening in the cliff, go to 30.

46

You suddenly realise that you have made a fatal mistake!

A stream of bullets rip into your body. You scream in pain before slipping into oblivion.

You have failed in your adventure.

If you wish to begin again, go to 1.

47

You open the door and carefully make your way down the empty corridor.

You turn a corner and see two armed men ahead of you. They appear to be standing guard outside a room. This room is obviously important!

You wonder what you should do.

If you wish to try to trick your way into the room, go to 14.

If you want to force the guards to let you into the room, go to 26.

If you decide to go back along the corridor, go to 28.

48

You follow Sukh out of the airport and into the car park where your jeep is waiting for you.

Sukh reaches forward, opens the door and then suddenly spins around.

You gasp – he is pointing a gun at your chest!

He gestures towards the open door. "Get in the car and do not make a sound," he orders. "Or it will go very badly with you."

If you try to resist being kidnapped, go to 2.
If you decide to do as he says, go to 28.

49

"How much are you offering?" you ask. "I will need to be paid a lot of money."

Greenback shakes his head. "You have failed my test. I want someone who values adventure and discovery more than money. You are not that person. Goodbye."

He marches out of the room. You realise that your greed has lost you the chance of taking part in a great adventure.

If you wish to begin again, go to 1.

50

"The Tomb of Temüjin will remain here undisturbed," you say. "And I promise that I will not betray this great secret."

The leader of the Guardians nods. "You have chosen wisely. I will order my people to escort you from our valley. To be a hero does not only mean doing brave deeds, but also making brave and noble choices. The choice you have made is a truly noble one and you are a true hero!"

QUIZ
TOMB RUNNER

YOU HAVE NOW COMPLETED YOUR MISSION. BUT CAN YOU RECALL THE KEY MOMENTS?
TAKE THIS QUIZ TO SEE HOW MUCH YOU CAN REMEMBER. THE ANSWERS ARE AT THE BACK OF THE BOOK. GOOD LUCK!

1 – What is the name of your butler?
a) Peters   b) Johnson
c) Roberts

2 – What is the name of the financier who wishes to hire you?
a) AC Richman   b) TJ Fatcat
c) JP Greenback

3 – Which empire was founded by Genghis Khan?
a) The Chinese Empire
b) The Roman Empire
c) The Mongol Empire

4 – What is the capital of Mongolia?
a) Beijing   b) Ulan Bator
c) Kathmandu

5 –   What is the name of the guide you are told
will meet you at the airport?
a) Jamuka   b) Hamula
c) Mamuta

6 –   Who actually meets you there?
a) Tükh   -   b) Sükh
c) Lükh

7 –   What creature attacks you as you try to
cross the underground lake?
a) a giant spider   b) a giant rat
c) a giant cockroach

8 –   What do you do to open the secret door in
the monastery library?
a) pull a secret lever
b) turn a prayer wheel
c) push a hidden button

9 –   Your enemies use a tracking device to
follow you – where is it hidden?
a) in your jeep   b) in your phone
c) in your pocket

10 - Who was Temüjin?
a) the captain of Genghis Khan's guard
b) Genghis Khan's wife
c) Genghis Khan's real name

ABOUT THE AUTHORS

"An irrepressibly brilliant team."

STEVE BARLOW and STEVE SKIDMORE are known as "THE 2 STEVES", the UK's most popular writing double act for young people, specialising in comedy and adventure.

THE 2 STEVES have been writing together for over twenty years - they have written over 220 books for young people and have also acted as series editors for major publishing houses.

THE 2 STEVES travel across the world to promote the importance and love of reading and to deliver writing masterclasses in schools and libraries, where their shows are described as "Hilarious... brilliant... and mad"!

BOOK SERIES by the 2 STEVES

iHero: Immortals
iHero: Toons
iHero: Monster Hunter
Monsters Like Us
Action Dogs
The Dark Forest
The Outernet
Dragonsdale

To find out more about "THE 2 STEVES", visit their website at www.the2steves.net

ANSWERS FOR SPACE RESCUE

1 – b   2 – c   3 – b   4 – a   5 – b   6 – a   7 – c   8 – c
9 – a   10 – b

SCORES:

8-10   GENIUS!
6-7   MORE BRAIN THAN BRAWN
3-5   MORE BRAWN THAN BRAIN
0-2   MORE ZERO THAN HERO!

ANSWERS FOR STRIKE FORCE

1 – c   2 – a   3 – a   4 – b   5 – c   6 – b   7 – a   8 – b
9 – a   10 – b

SCORES:

8-10   GENIUS!
6-7   MORE BRAIN THAN BRAWN
3-5   MORE BRAWN THAN BRAIN
0-2   MORE ZERO THAN HERO!

ANSWERS FOR TOMB RUNNER

1 – a   2 – c   3 – c   4 – b   5 – a   6 – b   7 – a   8 – b
9 – b   10 – c

SCORES:

8-10   GENIUS!
6-7   MORE BRAIN THAN BRAWN
3-5   MORE BRAWN THAN BRAIN
0-2   MORE ZERO THAN HERO!